Text and illustrations
© Alexa Saulino
Edited by Ariel Barnes

Order from www.frypiebooks.com

ISBN: 978-1-7364494-0-0

For A and B

One very **HOT** and **SUNNY** day the wind was blowing, and the grass was growing.

The grass stood as tall as it could to soak up all the **HOT** sun. The mama birds laid low in their shady nests with their babies.

There was a special house. In it was a lady, a man, a puppy, lots of house stuff, and some fries. Want to take a look inside?

Inside the house, the lady was in the kitchen eating some **HOT** fries and drinking some **HOT** coffee. She loved hot stuff.

She called out to the man upstairs, "Honey, you better come eat some fries while they're still hot!"

The lady was really hungry, but she managed to save 2 fries for the man upstairs. She had some stuff to do, so, she left them on the counter. She grabbed her bag, phone, lip balm, sunglasses, a drink, and then left the house.

The fries went from...

HOT to **KIND OF HOT** to **WARM** to **COLD**

Now, you see, most people don't know this, but I'll tell you a secret...

When fries get COLD, they WAKE UP!

They jump up right away and go on an adventure!

People love to blame their disappearing fries on babies, or dogs because they can't talk. But they just don't know
~The Way of the Fry~

Fries are creatures that just want to play ALL DAY. They are very sweet (wait, actually they are salty, and some more than others)! Yet, some are plain without any salt at all...

But they are all very nice.

All was quiet in the house until 1 fry started to WIGGLE! It was wiggling like crazy and then...

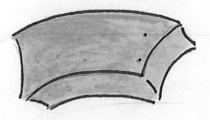

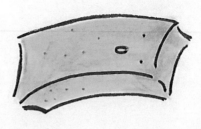

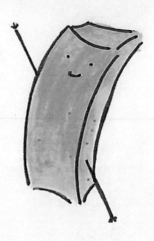

2 eyes appeared

then a mouth

1 skinny arm
and
1 skinny leg

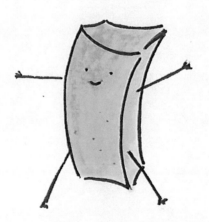

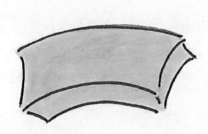

then the other
arm and leg

And it said, "Helloooo... wow...
where am I?"

The fry looked over and said, "Oh a
buddy, yay! Looks like it's not awake
though... I bet I can help with that!"

It looked down at its fry body and
saw sparkly crunchy noonies
everywhere and wondered what it was.

It was SALT!

So, we'll call him Salty.

The salty fry wanted to wake up its plain
friend, so, it started trying some super
silly stuff!

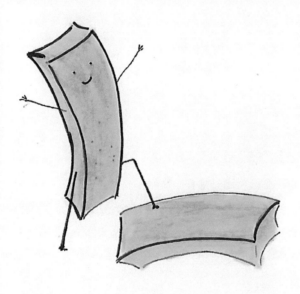 

First, it put its toes
on its friend and said,
"I bet you don't like my
stinky toes on you!

It found 2 old pieces
of rice and started
to make loud music
with them.

You better wake up and
tell me to stop!"

BANG! BANG! BANG!

Salty pretended the old rice was a phone.

"Hey, your granny is on the phone and she wants to speak with you right away! She wants to know what you want for your birthday!"

"Peekaboo!" Salty tried to surprise its friend.

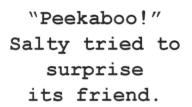

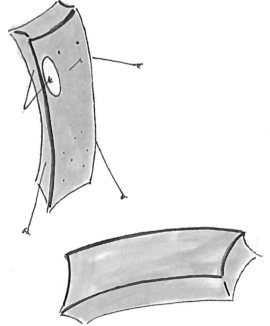

Then, they tried a wake-up race! Salty laid down and pretended they were sleeping.

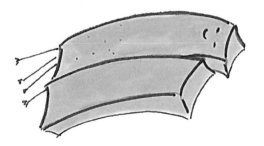

Nothing was working! What was Salty going to try next?

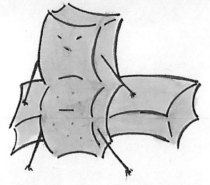

Salty thought, you really should
   be up already because
     you're really cold! I guess
      it just had to wait for the
       right time. It had a
        hard time being
         patient.

Then, the plain
fry started to
WIGGLE
   and out popped
     legs...
  a face...
arms...

and just
like that
it was up!

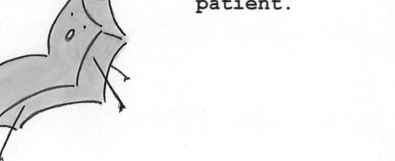

The salty fry looked at the plain fry and
was very pleased that it wasn't alone
anymore.

The plain fry was very excited and curious about their new world, and they were happy that they weren't alone in it.

The plain fry noticed that its friend was covered in sparkly crunchies and thought that they looked really cool.

It asked Salty where it got them from, but it wasn't sure. It was just born that way.

So, they decided to go on a best friend adventure and look for more of them.

The fries jumped up and hid behind the cookie jar.

They saw a big box on the other side of the counter and thought that would be a good place to look first.

It said SOAP BOX on it, but that wasn't very helpful because they hadn't learned to read yet.

They crept over to it very carefully...

They found a couple of old cookies and made some steps so they could get into the box. They were just little guys and needed some help.

The plain fry thought it would be a
good idea to know what Salty's noonies
tasted like, so, it asked its friend
if it could try a piece.

      Of course, Salty said, "Yes," and the
      plain fry really liked the taste.

            Then it thought, *Why do I think this*
            tastes like the ocean? Hey, what even
            is the ocean?!

Just before the plain fry jumped in the soap box, it paused
because it was a little scared...

Since there was a mouth on the
box maybe it was full
of TEETH!
or TOOTHPASTE!
or MOUTHS!

Then, it decided to be brave.
It took a deep breath and jumped in!

Maybe this was it!

The plain fry decided to taste what was inside
since it already knew what Salty's noonies
tasted like and could compare.

It got up and stood on Salty's head and jumped
into the box! Inside, it found a whole bunch
of crystals.

It picked up a tiny scoop and put it in its
mouth...

The plain fry quickly ran and jumped out of the soap box.

Then it said,
"YUCKKKKKK! Ewwwwwwww!"
It was not salt,
it was SOAP!
And soap does
NOT taste good!

All of that adventuring made those little fries
hungry, so they ran over to an apple and had a
few bites. Fries LOVE fruit.

Salty decided to play
around a bit on a lemon
wedge and work on
its balance.

"Ahhhhhhhh...
... Oooooohhhh!"

The fries heard some really tiny
footsteps, so they hid behind a HUGE
carrot.

They were really happy they found
that nice, big carrot to hide them.
They peeked out from over it.

Do you know what they saw?

A PUPPY!

She pushed over a chair and
jumped on it to try and look
at them!

> "Aww, a baby furry face,"
> said the plain fry.

"We better not get too
close. I bet she will lick
us like crazy!" said Salty.

> The fries decided they better
> get back to their mission.
> They blew the puppy some
> kisses and said goodbye.

Next, the fries came to a cup and they wanted to look inside of it.

Salty stood on a spoon and the plain fry
lifted it up so it could take a peek.

But Salty just saw some hot brown soup.

They wondered if they should jump
in for a swim, but decided to just
jump down and continue their important
mission as new best friends.

The fries were getting worried that they would never find more salt, and off in the distance they saw something else to look in.

They went over to the sugar bowl and grabbed the top. They pushed with all their might and threw it off!

Wow... this might finally be it, they thought.

It was full of sparkly noonies! The plain fry decided to do a taste test again. It took one tiny piece of sugar and put it into its tiny fry mouth and said,

"YUMMMM!"

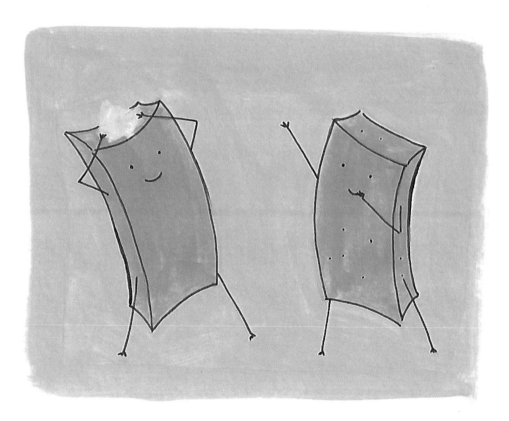

They were super happy that it tasted good even though it wasn't what they were looking for.

They liked it so much that they put a whole bunch on their head to save for later!

The fries had such an exciting day looking for salt, but now there wasn't anywhere else left to look in the kitchen.

They looked out the window and saw the big, beautiful sun sinking down getting ready to go to bed.

They didn't find salt today, but knew that if they kept trying, one day they would.

They walked to the edge of the counter and looked down. They saw a big basket of treasures that the lady called, "Trash."

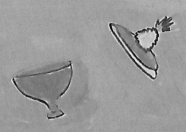

Something told them to JUMP IN.

They felt that in that big stinky pile of garbage that they would find all the answers, but they didn't know that it was stinky because they didn't have noses.

So, do you know what they did?

THEY JUMPED IN!

And just like that they started a new adventure together.

You don't always find what you're looking for.

Sometimes you find something even better.

CPSIA information can be obtained
at www.ICGtesting.com
Printed in the USA
BVRC091049290621
610252BV00001B/5

9 781736 449400